For the always insightful Danny.
—S.C.

To Wayne, Emily, and Amelia.
—E.U.

An imprint of Rodale Books
733 Third Avenue
New York, NY 10017
Visit us online at RodaleKids.com.

Rodale Kids books may be purchased for business or promotional use for special sales.
For information, please e-mail: RodaleKids@Rodale.com.

Printed in China
Manufactured by RRD Asia 201804

Design by Jeff Shake
Text set in Report School

The artwork for this book was created with pencil and paper, then painted digitally in Adobe Photoshop.
Library of Congress Cataloging-in-Publication Data is on file with the publisher.

ISBN 978-1-62336-957-6 paperback
ISBN 978-1-62336-959-0 hardcover

Distributed to the trade by Macmillan
10 9 8 7 6 5 4 3 2 1 paperback
10 9 8 7 6 5 4 3 2 1 hardcover

I am Smart

My alarm clock
wakes me up.
I get dressed and
go downstairs.

Mom made
my favorite breakfast—
egg-in-a-hole.
I am too nervous to eat.
I need to study.

I have a math test,
and one more review
will make me feel better.

Mom says, "You studied
last night. You got
a good night's sleep.
Now it's time
for brain food."

Mom is right!
I am prepared.
Now I am fueled up
and ready to go.
Breakfast was
a smart choice.

I am smart.
I've got this covered!

I feel hopeful all day until science class. Our teacher makes an announcement. We will have a science fair in two weeks.

I do not like science.
It is hard for me.
I worry about the fair
in gym class.

I worry about it
all the way home.

I am *still* worrying
about it at night.
Mom knows I struggle
in science class.
She encourages me
to pick something
I like or do every day.

"Look for the science
in your life," she says.

And just like that,
I get an idea.
It's a good idea.
It's a smart idea!

I jot down some notes
before I go to sleep.
I have so many questions.

I go to the library on Saturday.
First, I look up
information on my own.

Next, I ask the librarian.
"You ask very smart
questions," he says.

Over the next few days,
I read about gravity and
how it flips a bottle.
I learn how weight,
shape, and speed
affect the bottle.

I make a lot of noise and
it gets a little messy.

Then I spend a few days
trying different setups.
I add different amounts
of water to the bottles.

I try bigger bottles
and smaller bottles.
Chance and Taylor stop by.
They want to play soccer.

But I don't want to
stop working on my experiment.
My experiment is fun.
I show my friends.
I ask them for help.

They stay and have fun.
I made a smart choice.

Our teacher gives us
permission to work
together!

We record the results.

We make posters.

We practice doing demonstrations.

Finally, the science fair is here.
I am nervous and excited.
We answer everyone's
questions.

Our experiment works!

THE EFFECT OF
DIFFERENT WATER
AMOUNTS USED FOR
BOTTLE FLIPPING

It is time
to hand out prizes.
Chance, Taylor, and I
cross our fingers
and link arms.

We win a prize
for best demonstration.
We flip out!

I worked hard.
I asked for help.
Chance, Taylor, and I
celebrate with sundaes.

I learned a lot
about bottle flipping,
science, and myself.
I am smart.

When do YOU feel smart?

Can you think of three examples?

Also available:

I Am Helpful

Look for these other titles in the
POSITIVE POWER series:

- • I Am Thankful
- • I Am Kind
- • I Am Brave
- • I Am Strong

To learn more about Rodale Kids Curious Readers,
please visit RodaleKids.com.